ESEA
TITLE I

Dad and Me in the Morning

Dad and Me in the Morning

Patricia Lakin

Illustrated by Robert G. Steele

ALBERT WHITMAN & COMPANY • MORTON GROVE, ILLINOIS

The illustrations are in watercolor.
The text is set in Bembo Medium.
Design by Karen Johnson Campbell.

Text ©1994 by Patrica Lakin Koeningsberg.
Illustrations ©1994 by Robert G. Steele.
Published in 1994 by Albert Whitman & Company,
6340 Oakton Street, Morton Grove, Illinois 60053-2723.
Published simultaneously in Canada by
General Publishing, Limited, Toronto.
Printed in the United States of America.
10 9 8 7 6 5 4

Library of Congress Cataloging-In-Publication Data
Lakin, Patricia.
Dad and me in the morning/ by Patricia Lakin;
illustrated by Robert Steele.
p. cm.
Summary: A deaf boy and his father share a special time as they
watch the sunrise at the beach.
ISBN 0-8075-1419-5
[1. Fathers and sons—Fiction. 2. Deaf—Fiction. 3. Physically
handicapped—Fiction. 4. Morning—Fiction. 5. Seashore—Fiction.]
I. Steele, Robert, ill. II. Title
PZ7.L1586Dad 1994   93-36169
[E]—DC20   CIP
                                                                      AC

For Lee, who took me to see the sunrise.
With special thanks to Mildred Oberkotten for her insight. —P. L.

To my wife, Alice; my daughter, Catherine; and my son, Tyler,
for constant patience and inspiration. —R. G. S.

My special alarm clock flashed.

I shut it off quickly and sat up!

My little brother was still asleep. Good! It was dark everywhere.

I slid out of bed, put on my hearing aids and my clothes, and took my flashlight.

Then I tiptoed down the long hall.

I inched my way to Dad's side of the bed and gave him a little shake.

I flicked on my flashlight so I could read his lips. He opened an eye.

"I'm ready," he said. Then he scratched his head.

"Don't wake anybody," I warned him.

"I'll be quiet," he said. And I knew he would. When we can't make noise, like now, or in the movies, Dad just mouths the words. But I can speech-read, so I know what he's saying.

"Okay," I signed. "Hurry!"

I slid down the bannister and waited by the front door.

Finally! I could feel the clomp of Dad's feet coming down the stairs.

"Come on," I signed. "I don't want to miss it."

He held out my sweatshirt.

I opened the door. Everything looked grey. And cold air hit my face.

"Warm enough, Jacob?" I watched him sign.

"Sure." I zipped up my sweatshirt and held onto his hand.

Dad and I have lots of ways of talking to each other, like signing or lipreading or just squeezing each other's hands. That's our secret signal.

We walked down the dirt road that led to the beach.

"Nobody's up but us," said Dad.

"He is!" I pointed to a baby bunny sitting near the flowers. He looked right at me. Then he jumped and hid under a big branch.

I took a deep breath. "I love the smell of pine trees."

"It's the peacefulness I like." Dad squeezed my hand.

I squeezed back. And I walked so my feet could feel the hard slap, slapping of my sandals.

I kicked them off when we got to the beach.
I ran barefoot into the water.
"Cold!" I shouted, and ran right out.

"It's getting lighter," I told Dad. "We didn't miss it, did we?"

"No, but it's almost time."

"Where do we go to see it?"

Dad pointed to the huge rocks way at the other end of the beach.

"Follow me!" I yelled.

I made Dad run over the hard sand, through the crunchy shells, and over the snaky seaweed, right to the rocks.

We climbed onto a nice flat one and sat side by side.

I held my nose. "These wet rocks smell like old, stinky fish," I told Dad. Then something tickled my leg. "Hermit crabs!"

We watched them scoot into a crack.

"Now is it time?" I asked.

He checked his watch. "In three and a half minutes. Look right there." Dad pointed way out, over the water.

I stared at the line where the water touches the sky. But nothing was happening. So I looked around.

I saw a seagull drop a shell onto the rocks. He swooped down and gobbled the insides. Then he took off. That's when I saw them . . .

"There!" I told Dad. I pointed behind us to the
clouds. They looked like popcorn. They were

turning pink and purple and orange and yellow.
And the sky was getting more and more blue.

Dad tapped my shoulder. "Look there," he said.
I turned. I didn't think it would be like that...

just an eensy slice of orange peeking up out of the water.

"Wow!" In seconds, it got bigger and bigger and
kept floating, up and up and up . . . getting brighter
and warmer and orangier and rounder.

"It's gigantic and so close!" I said. "I wish I could touch it."

Dad gave me a big hug.

"Let's come back here," I signed. "Just you and me."

"Love to," Dad signed.

Then I looked up again. But the brightness hurt my eyes.

So I leaned against Dad, closed my eyes, and let the sun warm my face.